WARNING

This book contains sexually explicit scenes and adult language. It may be considered offensive to some readers. This book is for sale to adults ONLY.

* * * * * * * * * * * * * * * * *

Please store your files wisely where they cannot be accessed by underage readers.

ISBN-13: 978-1987863512
ISBN-10: 1987863518

Other books by Shyla Starr:

<u>Persuasive Billionaire BWWM Romance Series</u>

Stacey is trying to keep a handle on her life the best that she can. She is on the verge of losing her job and her apartment, while taking care of her sick grandmother. Her life takes an unexpected turn when she meets Charlie, who works for the construction company that is attempting to persuade her to move out of her home.

<u>Tenacious Billionaire BWWM Romance Series</u>

Adalia is too proud to accept help from the billionaire playboy, Trent Dawson. How long can she maintain her resolve? The bank is at her heels to repossess her business. To make matters worse, Adalia finds suspicious evidence of Trent's philandering ways. She must determine whether to trust Trent with the fate of her business and her heart.

<u>Elusive Billionaire Romance Series</u>

Billionaire Hendrick is trying to repair his company's image by putting in some volunteer work, building a school and hospital for the impoverished children in Africa. There, he meets a beautiful African American volunteer, Jocelyn. They hit it off right away but does she belong in his world?

<u>Lonely Billionaire Romance Series</u>

Tricia was hired to care for billionaire John's wife, who is dying. An unlikely romance emerges after his wife, Rebecca, gives John permission to pursue his happiness after she is gone.

<u>Ardent Billionaire Romance Series</u>

Deirdre doesn't know what to make of the gorgeous man that seems to be interested in her. His name is Parker Walters and he seems friendly enough. There is just something off about him. Why is he trying the hide the fact that he is the heir to his father's billion dollar software empire?

<u>Fervent Billionaire BWWM Romance Series</u>

Alexandra had never been with a white man before. She had seen William at the café before but she always kept her distance. It was unfortunate that their first chance meeting happened when she dropped her breakfast and spilled coffee all over his expensive business suit.

Get the latest update on new releases from the author at:

https://shylastarr.com/newsletter/

This book is Part One of the "Audacious Billionaire BWWM Romance Series"

1 - Love Eluded

Chante is torn between staying close to a man beyond her league, and fleeing from him to spare herself from a hopeless position. But she finds she is propelled into a place where she needs to confront her doubts and cast her fate aside to follow the dictates of her heart. Damned if she does and miserable is she doesn't, how will Chante face the events that will lead her to a place of pure happiness or to the pits of a broken heart?

2 - Love Astray

Chante is slowly getting over her heartbreak from the enigmatic Jared Lowell. Realizing that he is not the right man for her, she is ready to fall in love again and finds happiness once more in the arms of her new lover, Dr. Leo Cadman. That is until Jared's presence at the hospital stirs up all the emotions she used to have for him. Torn between the affections of a man who adores her and a sexual attraction she cannot contradict, who will Chante gamble her heart with?

3 - Love Abided

Chante finds herself accepting a marriage proposal from a man everybody considers 'the perfect man'. She knows she is the luckiest woman on earth. But although she could fool everyone else, she could never fool herself. Her heart belongs to Jared Lowell. It always had since the day she first laid eyes on him. Caught between a farce of an engagement and a growing intimacy between her and Jared, which will win in the battle for the truth... her heart or her mind?

Audacious Billionaire BWWM Romance Series

Love Eluded

Book One

By Shyla Starr

Table of Contents

Chapter One

CHANTE GREEN knew she was going to be late for work…again.

"Shit…," she mumbled, impatiently tapping her foot as she craned her neck to see if the bus was anywhere in sight.

She could almost see the look of annoyance on the face of her supervisor, Nurse Betty Lebowitz. It was the third time this month alone and Chante knew she was hanging by a thread. She could lose her job at New York General Hospital, and she needed that now more than ever.

Chante genuinely hoped that Nurse Betty would be a little sympathetic and cut her some slack. After all, the supervisor was familiar with the reason Chante was under a tremendous amount of pressure. Her brother Markey had ALS or Amyotrophic Lateral Sclerosis, also known as Lou Gehrig's disease.

A catastrophic disease that was initially misdiagnosed, Markey now had only partial control of his legs. Looking back, he was always clumsy as a child, often falling or stumbling, but everyone said it was just a phase and he'll eventually outgrow it. But as the years progressed, Chante noticed the slurred speech.

Her mom eventually took him to a specialist who, after rigorous testing declared the boy was in the second stages of ALS.

Things became even more difficult when Chante's dad contracted malaria and eventually died from it. Chante and her mom, both heartbroken over the sudden death, struggled to meet the special needs that were required to deal with ALS. Her mom, having had experience in caring for sick children, took on most of the responsibilities. When swallowing became too hard, they took turns giving him food through a feeding tube. Mom would bathe him; help him use the bathroom; exercise his arms and legs to prevent atrophy, until her son's disease took its toll on her as well.

Driving one night to buy medicine at a nearby pharmacy, she was too preoccupied to notice the red light at a street intersection and was hit on the driver's side by a passing truck. She was in a coma for three days before she succumbed to her injuries. At nineteen years old, Chante was left with an enormous responsibility towards a brother who was not even of her own blood, but who meant more to her than anything in the whole world. He was her only family.

Chante didn't remember much of her early childhood years, except shuttling from one foster home to another. At six years old, she was considered too old by most couples wanting to adopt a baby. The shy and gawky black girl with soulful green eyes was never chosen. Unable to find a good family for her, city officials decided to turn her over to the State Institution for Unwanted Children. On the eve of her departure, a woman came in, noticed her cringing in a corner, and approached her.

Chante believed she was an angel with blond hair falling softly around her shoulder. But it was the sweet voice that calmed her enough to reach for the hand that was offered to her. The woman was enamored with the emaciated child and decided to adopt her. The lady, Hannah Green, brought her home and introduced her to her husband, Caleb, a Mulatto who was delighted to see her. Chante felt an instant kinship with the dark-skinned stranger. Hannah made her feel like the daughter they never had. Both were missionaries who went to far-flung places on medical missions.

Chante spent her growing years travelling to places most children would have found depressing. No electricity, no running water, and sometimes just a hut to sleep on at night, if they were lucky. Otherwise, it had to be in a tent or under the stars. Children with malaria, TB, pneumonia, measles, and countless other maladies constantly filled their days.

From her adoptive parents, Chante learned compassion, dedication, and sympathy for the sick. No one was turned away. There was always room for one more.

Chante blossomed under their care. The lost look in her eyes gradually changed to confidence. She learned her ABC's under Acacia trees with other children. Instead of children's books, medical books were her constant companion. She couldn't read most of the words, but the pictures amazed her. It was no surprise that she declared she would become a doctor someday. She changed her mind after she found her passion working alongside the nurses, who took care of their patients day in and day-out.

It was during one of these missions that her mom and dad discovered that they were expecting a baby. Chante's innate insecurity returned. She knew she was adopted and was afraid to be given away again. Her parents, seeing the troubled look on her face, assured her that she would always be a part of their family. They loved her so much like she was their very own, they said. That restored her confidence so much so that when the baby finally arrived, Chante immediately fell in love with the little bundle of crinkly skin and puffy eyes. No one seeing them for the first time would ever doubt they were brother and sister. They looked so much alike… same curly hair and bronzed chocolaty skin complexion.

When Chante's dad contracted malaria and eventually died from it, they moved to a smaller house. Maintaining the big sprawling colonial house where Chante grew up became too much for her mom. Money was scarce with the little pension she was receiving from her work as a missionary and Chante was in her last year in high school.

They found a modest apartment in Queen's where they had better access to local facilities and clinics for her brother Markey. They joined a local chapter for ALS victims trying to understand and cope with their situation at home.

Chante remembered her childhood passion of becoming a nurse, her caring disposition making her a natural. She looked into the idea of nursing school and found work as a candy striper in a hospital nearby. She enjoyed the experience of helping care for the sick. Her duties revolved around making a patient's stay in the hospital more pleasant. She delivered the patients' meals, helped feed them, occasionally read to them, and assisted in releasing them from the hospital. When the nurses found themselves overburdened, Chante gladly took on more responsibilities.

Everyone who knew Chante was fond of her. Chante Green was an attractive girl with a heart of gold. She cared for her patients and treated them like they were family. Friends who knew her well concluded this was her way of giving back. She had found her purpose and it gave her the experience to deal with her own personal situation at home with Markey.

After six months of volunteer work, she decided to take a course as a Certified Nursing Assistant after her Volunteer Coordinator assured her of a paying job at New York General Hospital. Chante was elated. She signed up for a three month night-course when her mom met the accident that took her life away.

Chante never fully grasped where she got the strength to carry on. Those days were like dark clouds hovering over her head ready to engulf her in an instant. Making the funeral arrangements so soon after her dad's passing, talking to Markey and making him understand that it was just the two of them from now on, and trying to cope with her CNA classes… there were lots of instances when Chante just wanted to give up. She often cried herself to sleep, burying her head in her pillow so Markey wouldn't hear her moaning with grief. The enormity of what lay ahead was just too much for a young girl and she was often just very scared about the future.

Thankfully, the ALS organization came to her rescue. They assisted her in every way they could until Chante got back the determination to continue. She eventually finished the three months CNA course and landed her current job at New York General Hospital.

"Oh, thank God," Chante whispered in relief as she spotted the silver-gray public transport that would bring her to work with hardly any minute to spare. The bus was less than two blocks away, lumbering slowly beside the sidewalk, picking up riders as they waited. Chante made sure her ID was in her bag, as well as her cell phone. She needed to be able to keep in touch with Liza, the caregiver who was currently with Markey. She was the reason Chante was running late. Liza called in an hour ago and told Chante she was held up at home with an emergency.

Chante panicked, knowing that she couldn't afford to miss work, but Liza thought she was only going to be a half-hour late. If Chante could hold on, she'd be there, she promised. Markey was seated in the living room watching his favorite cartoon. It always broke her heart seeing him with a blanket across his legs. He should be out playing basketball or hanging out with his friends, Chante thought.

"Hey Chant," Markey called out when he spotted her checking in on him, "You off to work now?"

"Soon as Liza comes. She said she'll be a half-hour late today," Chante replied.

"I can manage. It doesn't look like I'll be going anywhere," Markey replied with a naughty grin.

Chante approached her brother and tousled his hair. She knew he hated that. "I know, but I'll feel better knowing that you're with someone," Chante countered.

"You worry too much about me. I'll be fine…," Markey reassured her.

Chante let out a sigh and replied, "I know kid, we both will." As soon as Liza knocked, Chante gave her brother a peck on the cheek and ran out the door.

"C'mon…c'mon…," Chante urged the bus that was still a half a block away. She was so intent on making the bus go faster that she hardly noticed a figure approaching slowly from behind until the man put his arm across her shoulder.

"How's my favorite girl… I haven't seen you in a while," the man said.

Chante gave a surprise shriek at the sudden contact, swiveled around and saw who it was. "Jimmy…," she gasped with relief, thankful it wasn't a mugger. And then as Jimmy's presence dawned on her, a sudden fear crept inside her chest. She had been trying to avoid

Jimmy Derollo for weeks now. She didn't answer his calls, hoping he would get the message and stop. He was the last person on Earth that she wanted to see now that she was in a rush to get to work.

"Jimmy…I'm in a real big hurry right now. I can't stay and talk…," Chante said stiffly as she struggled to get away from the arm that was still across her shoulder.

"Hey… hey… hey… aren't you even glad to see me?" Jimmy asked with a nasty sneer.

Chante knew better than to antagonize him. Jimmy Derollo was a shady character that lived in the same neighborhood. He had a Mohawk haircut dyed in purple shade and a nose ring. He wore a black leather jacket with skin tight jeans and leather boots. Before she knew better, Chante thought he was cool. This was the period in Chante's life when she didn't know what to do and where to go. Her mom's death left her confused and terrified. When she met Jimmy, he seemed eager to know more about her and she ended up telling him about her troubles. Jimmy was all ears and a shoulder to cry on. Chante found his attention gratifying and thought she found a rock to hold on to in her very confusing world.

They went out on a few dates until one day she ended up in his apartment. He passed her a joint and assured her it was alright. Chante never smoked pot in all her life. She coughed and sputtered, unable to catch her breath. She really thought she was choking to death until the effect of the drug hit her. From then on, she was like putty in his hands. They had sex right on the couch with Chante a captive participant, unable to resist. She just remembered feeling lifeless with no control over her arms as Jimmy pounded into her repeatedly. She woke up a couple of hours later, naked, on his bed, with Jimmy snoring away next to her.

Chante felt pain all over her body. She had no memory of what had transpired between them. An overwhelming sense of shame swept through her entire being. She didn't need to remember anything at all. Her imagination more than made up for what she didn't know. She saw him a couple times more and each time they were together, Chante realized exactly just how bad a decision she made thinking he was special. Jimmy was not only into drugs. He was also a convicted felon out on parole for extortion. Chante always believed in giving people second chances, but instinctively she knew Jimmy Derollo didn't belong in that category.

Chante looked around helplessly. Jimmy, seeing the confused look on her face, made a move and came even closer. He held a hand out to her chin and raised her head to kiss her. Chante turned her head away at just the right time for his kiss to land on the side of her face. Chante didn't know what possessed her as she let a resounding slap land on his face.

"What the fuck…," Jimmy said as he grimaced in pain. He made a move to grab her by the shoulder as the bus rolled to a stop in front of them. The automatic doors hissed open and a voice hailed out to them.

"Miss…is that man bothering you. I can use my radio and call 911…," the voice of the driver called out loudly.

Jimmy let go of her arm immediately. He was on parole and didn't need this right now.

"It's alright…I'm ok…," Chante replied, knowing that for now at least she was safe from Jimmy. She immediately moved towards the safety of the bus door.

Jimmy gave her a sinister look as he muttered under his breath, "this ain't over yet, bitch… I have something on you that you don't know about."

Chante was still within earshot to hear the threat in his voice, but she didn't stand around to know what was behind it. She had to get to work and away from this disgusting man who, unfortunately, was an ex-boyfriend. She resolved to momentarily forget about Jimmy and focus on the next eight hours of her shift.

Chante reached the back entrance to the hospital and headed straight for the rows of gray metal lockers in the basement, entered the ladies bathroom and donned her uniform. She studied her reflection in the wall mirror, splashed cold water on her face, and removed a tube of toothpaste and brushed her teeth vigorously. Strands of hair entangled around her nape. She took a moment to comb her dark hair back into a severe bun. Reaching for the light switch, she turned it off and opened the door to the hallway leading to the Nurse's Station on the second floor.

Amos, the hospital janitor was removing bleach from the closet when he saw her. "Good Morning, Ms. Chante. You shoo is a sight for tired eyes," Amos greeted her.

"Good morning, Amos. What's the floor like today? Should I hide from Nurse Betty?" Chante replied back gaily.

"Oh, I think she'll hardly notice you're late agin. B'sides, she should give you some slack, coz of that lil' brother of yours and everythin'…," the old man replied.

"I surely hope so, Amos. But I'm at the bottom of the food chain. So…," Chante replied with a grin.

"I did see Nurse Betty few hours ago and she look like them chicken that got its head chop' off and hadn't made the connection," Amos informed her.

Chante laughed out loud. "Why… what's causing the buzz this time?" Chante asked curiously.

The hospital was always on heightened alert. Chante had already accepted that as part of hospital life.

"Oh…I dunno… some bigwig came in a helicopter…set the whole place in a-tizzy. Some rich folk, I reckon…," Amos answered with a shake of his head. He had been working in the hospital a long time that nothing ever ruffled him.

"Well, alright then…," said Chante, waving as she hurried to report to the head supervisor. She sincerely hoped Amos was right and Nurse Betty wouldn't notice she was five minutes late.

"Chante…" A voice hailed her as she turned a corner of the hospital wing. Glancing around, she recognized Debbie, an intern recently assigned to her wing.

"Hi Debbie," greeted Chante.

"Have you heard…?" Debbie asked. She knew everything happening within the many walls of NYGH. She made it her business.

"Heard what… I just arrived for work. I expect to get another lecture from Nurse Betty about the ethics of coming in early. I'm late again, you know," Chante explained, hoping that Debbie would take the hint and let her go. Debbie wrinkled her nose. She knew what that was like. Suddenly she remembered why she was so excited and the sparkle returned to her eyes.

"Guess who was just brought in early this morning. You'll never guess in a hundred years…," Debbie challenged.

Chante knew Debbie was raring to tell. So she shrugged her shoulders and said, "Who?"

"Mrs. Samantha Lowell. The mother of *the* Jared Lowell," Debbie answered with a girlish shriek.

The name didn't register and Chante's face showed it. "Who is Jared Lowell," a clueless Chante asked. She was certain that Debbie would give her the rundown even if she wasn't that interested to know. A patient was a patient regardless of status. That much she learned from her adoptive parents.

"Duh… just the richest man alive, the most sought after bachelor in the whole America," Debbie replied, hardly believing that Chante didn't recognize the name.

"You've never heard of him?" she asked in disbelief.

"Nope… sorry… Forbes Magazine is not a guilty pleasure," Chante replied with a laugh. She imagined a balding man with a beer belly, smoking a cigar and dressed in fancy $500 suits. "What's the mother here for?" Chante was curious to know.

"Ohhh…according to the grapevine, Mrs. Lowell suffered from chest pains late last night. Their family physician suggested that she be brought to the hospital. But apparently Mrs. Lowell refused, saying she was just tired. The doctor thought otherwise and called her son, Jared Lowell, who was in Geneva and flew in by private jet to be by his mom's side. She was airlifted here via their private helicopter," Debbie narrated, her eyes glowing with excitement.

"Oh, Chante, but he is absolutely gorgeous… ohhh… I hope I get assigned to watch over his mom…," said Debbie, drooling.

"Good luck then…" Chante waved her off, forgetting in an instant everything she heard from her. And then Debbie added, "Nurse Betty is losing her mind. The General Director has been on her case since the chopper landed. Seems like they're undermanned right now, what with four other nurses being on sick leave and all…"

Chante realized that the sooner she announced her arrival, the higher the chances that Nurse Betty would let her tardiness today slip by. She was right.

"Oh Chante… I'm so glad you're here. I need you to fill out these forms. I just don't have the time for that right now," Nurse Betty said as she handed Chante a huge stack of papers.

"Alright," Chante replied as she heaved a sigh of relief.

"And don't think I haven't noticed that you're late again," Nurse Betty said with a disapproving look on her face. "You should be so lucky I need all hands on deck today."

"Of course, Nurse Betty," Chante replied with chagrin. She should have known that the supervisor had always one eye on the clock.

Chapter Two

Chante spent the next couple of hours filing documents and transporting medical records to the appropriate hospital departments. She checked on the insurance liabilities of the patients on record and made sure everything was up-to-date. It was mostly clerical work that she used to do as a candy striper. She didn't mind though because she wanted to be useful while she was on duty.

Occasionally, Nurse Betty would hand her a couple of lab specimens and requests for drugs from the pharmacy. Before she knew it, her eight hour shift was over and she had a crick in the back of her neck from all the paperwork she did.

She stretched out her tired body and was about to head for the exit when Nurse Betty came running down the hallway.

"Listen, honey… I know you just came out of an 8-hour shift, but do you mind doing another 3 hours more? We're seriously understaffed right now," Nurse Betty explained.

Chante was eager to leave and see Markey before he went to bed. But Nurse Betty had a pleading look on her face. Chante realized that this was an occasion to get on her good side.

"Alright, Nurse Betty… let me call home and check on Markey… see if Liza can ask someone to replace her. I'll join you in a while," Chante replied with a smile. Nurse Betty smiled in relief. She knew Chante never declined a request. She always came through.

Nurse Betty was busy checking on patients' charts, updating reports, and giving out assigned posts when Chante walked back in.

"Chante, I'm glad you're here," she said, while pulling a chart from the bottom of the pile. She lowered her voice and ushered her away from the other nurses hovering around the station.

"I've assigned you to Suite 247," Nurse Betty informed her. Chante was surprised. Suite 247 was reserved mostly for celebrities, government officials, dignitaries, and other prominent people; it was a hotly contested commodity among the nurses. She glanced at the name on the chart and read 'LOWELL, SAMANTHA' written in big bold letters. The name sounded familiar. And then she realized this was the person Debbie was talking about early this morning. Well… it was the son she was drooling about mostly.

Nurse Betty saw the surprised look on her face and said, "Well… are you going to start slobbering like all the other idiot nurses? Goddammit… you'd think these bitches have never seen a handsome face before. Nurse Ruth dropped a bedpan… that new girl Debbie mistook a benzo for a vitamin pill… giggling and tittering like a bunch of hormonal school girls. I'm surprised Mr. Lowell hasn't called Director Whittle yet."

Nurse Betty sighed in exasperation and said, "Please, Chante… I've had a full day trying to make do with these foolish nurses and their raging hormones. I just need a reading… pulse, temp, etc… you know the drill."

"Yes… of course, I can manage that," Chante reassured the supervisor. Chante's rubber-soled shoes shuffled soundlessly towards the room where a 'STRICTLY NO VISITORS ALLOWED' sign hung. She opened the door and entered.

The suite was huge compared to the other rooms in the hospital. Curtains were drawn tightly over glass windows. Darkness was dispelled by the warm light of a bedside lamp. A custom made retractable black and silver bed that looked like it belonged in a five star hotel, was pushed into the rear wall between the closed windows. Tucked neatly with a quilt up to her a waist was a woman silently reading a book. She held up a forefinger to her lips indicating that Chante should be quiet.

From the glow of the reading lamp beside her, Chante saw that the woman had silver-gray hair that fell to her shoulder. Her regal bearing was complemented by grayish-blue eyes under perfectly arched brows, a small patrician nose, and thinning lips.

"Mrs. Lowell, I'm Chante. I didn't mean to disturb you. I just need to make some readings and then I'll be out of here again," Chante explained softly.

"It's all right my dear, I needed some company anyway. We just need to be quiet. My son is asleep. The poor boy had been up the last 24 hours worrying about me," Mrs. Lowell explained.

Chante nodded as she glanced at a smaller bed a few feet away. This must be Jared Lowell, the man who had set the hospital nurses on fire. Chante did not see anything except a hulking figure. That side of the room was in semi-darkness.

She took the old woman's temperature and pulse reading and said, "Everything looks normal. Can I do anything for you before I go?"

"Well…I really need to… pee," Mrs. Lowell answered.

Chante recognized the look of embarrassment on her face. Somebody with her pedigree probably felt awkward asking assistance for such a personal need. She entered the bathroom and saw a bedpan and carried it towards the bed.

"Uhmm… what's that?" the old woman asked, with what sounded like horror in her voice.

"It's a bedpan," Chante replied, feeling foolish.

Of course it was a bedpan.

"I know it's a bedpan. But why are you bringing it to me?" Mrs. Lowell asked.

"You said you wanted to pee," Chante replied with some confusion.

"I'm not peeing on any bedpan," the old lady declared, as she struggled to get out of bed.

Chante nearly dropped the bedpan as she jumped across the room to stop her.

"You can't get out of bed…," she said as she tried to push her back.

"I can if I want to pee… and I'm not peeing on a tin can…," the old lady answered obstinately.

"Alright, I'll help you…. but please take it easy. You can have a dizzy spell after being in bed," Chante replied as she took hold of the old woman's arm.

"What the fuck do you think you're doing?" a voice called out from the other side.

Chante was taken aback and looked in the direction where the voice came from. As the figure rose and emerged from darkness, Chante barely suppressed a gasp. And as he approached nearer, Chante caught her breath. If she didn't exhale soon she'd turn blue in the face.

The man was stunning. Brownish-blond hair over a chiseled face, thick brows over cobalt-blue eyes, a finely sculpted nose, high cheekbones, and a good strong jaw line. A slight flaw of a cleft chin only managed to enhance the Adonis effect.

The buttons on the rumpled shirt was open all the way, revealing a smooth hairless chest. Portions of a six-pack lay visible against the narrow opening. He was barefoot and Chante thought that she had never seen more perfectly formed toes in all her life.

The upper part of his pants hung low over a narrow waist and Chante had to exert all her strength of mind and body not to stare at the swelling that was etched against the crotch of his pants.

"Oh my God!!!" Chante's heart skipped a beat as she clamped her mouth shut.

If this man managed to wake up each time with that erection, he should be considered a lethal weapon. Now she understood what the brouhaha was all about.

"I-We…," was all she managed to say.

"Oh, don't get your panties in a bunch, Jared. Chante was just helping me get to the bathroom," Mrs. Lowell admonished her son.

You're not supposed to be out of bed…," Jared replied, giving Chante an annoyed look like it was her fault.

"I can if I want to go to the bathroom," his mom answered, glaring up at him.

Chante was caught between mother and son locked in a battle of will.

"Oh…alright," he conceded as he came near to take his mom's arm.

"Chante can manage…Can't you, dear?" the old lady asked as she pushed her son away.

Chante managed to nod her head mutely. Samantha Lowell's remark about the panties in a bunch somehow managed to steady her equilibrium. She tried to dismiss the image from her mind and the laughter that was slowly forcing its way up her throat.

But the problem with trying to overcome one's laughter in an absurd situation is that the more it persists on being set free.

Chante felt her body heave as she let out a slight titter hoping to release the funny sensation inside her head.

"I'm sorry…," she managed to whisper to the old woman as she guided her towards the toilet.

"It's quite alright, my dear, sometimes he needs to be put in his place," replied Mrs. Lowell, tapping her arm slightly.

Chante kept her back to Jared Lowell as his mom entered the cubicle. It wouldn't do to let him see the amusement on her face.

"Well…don't just stand there like a statue. It usually takes her a while to finish her absolution," Jared remarked from behind.

Absolution…really? Couldn't he just say pee? Chante kept a straight face.

She squared her shoulders, determined to stay where she was. She had a job to do and if it meant staying by the door till Mrs. Lowell finished with her absolution, so be it.

After a few seconds more, Jared added, "You look like an ass standing there by the door."

"At least my panties are not in a bunch…," Chante remarked, before she actually realized she said that out loud.

A stunned silence followed. Then she actually heard the man snicker before she got the courage to slowly turn around and face him.

"You are a feisty one, aren't you?" Jared remarked, standing just a few feet away from where she stood at her post.

Chante found his proximity stimulating and unsettling at the same time.

"Look Mr. Lowell…," Chante began.

"Jared…," he cut in.

"Jared…err… Mr. Lowell, I'm here on orders to look after…," Chante continued.

"I know…I know…," said Jared, cutting in once more.

Then he did a totally unexpected thing. He moved even closer until they were just inches away from one another.

"You understand my concern, don't you?" he asked, with an earnest look on his face.

Chante didn't realize that she could go beyond unsettled. *This…* was unsettling on the verge of panic. She felt like a deer caught between the headlights of on an oncoming car. Well… her eyes were just as startled as she tried to lower her lids to prevent them from blinding him as well.

And it didn't help any that he reached out a finger to her chin and raised her face to meet his.

Chante never understood the overwhelming desire that washed over her. Instinctively, she opened her lips as if waiting to be kissed. Jared's arm snaked its way behind her ass, copped a feel, before pulling her even closer.

Chante could at this time feel the hard authenticity of the bulge that earlier was just a figment of her imagination.

She closed her eyes as if in dream waiting for the kiss that was about to come. Then through her fogged brain, she heard the water flushing from inside the toilet, which brought her back to reality. Her eyes flew open in a snap.

"Gotcha…," Jared mocked as he released her.

Chante was stunned, shocked, and then mortified.

This man just played her. And she fell hook, line, and sinker.

Just then, the door to the suite opened and Nurse Betty entered with the Hospital Director, Jonathan Whittle, behind her.

He announced that he was there to accompany Mrs. Lowell to have her MRI done.

"Is that really necessary?" Samantha Lowell protested.

"It's just part of a series of tests that I want you to undergo. We must rule out all possibilities of a heart condition," Director Lowell answered in a condescending voice.

The four of them, the Director, Nurse Betty, Mrs. Lowell and her son, discussed briefly as Chante stayed rooted to the spot.

"Oh, alright…," said the old woman. "But please let Chante stay. I will need her after the procedure. This isn't going to take too long, is it?" She asked Nurse Betty impatiently.

Nurse Betty shook her head in response to the question. Chante took it to mean that she was not allowed to stay, so she headed awkwardly for the door.

"Stay!" The director barked at her.

A wheelchair was brought in to ferry Mrs. Lowell to the third floor and Chante hurriedly positioned herself behind it, ready to push the old woman out of the room.

"I said stay!" the director reiterated.

Chante was starting to feel like a dog having difficulty understanding her master's command.

She meekly let go of the chair and moved out of the way as the procession headed out the door. Unfortunately, it didn't include the son who had a wicked grin on his face.

If she could make herself disappear, she would, but she didn't dare leave the room until the old woman returned.

She set about tidying up the bed trying her best to ignore the presence of Jared Lowell.

"You really don't have to do that," he proclaimed as he plopped onto the pillow she was trying to smooth out.

Chante jumped back, startled. Her sense of dignity was being trampled and he was really starting to annoy her.

"Humph…," Chante retorted allowing her irritation to show. She didn't care. He was being obnoxious and she wanted him to know it.

Thankfully, no one was around to witness her momentary faux pas. Chante struggled to retrieve her professional demeanor, reached for the patient's chart and made a pretense of studying it. She didn't even notice he had gotten out of the bed and was standing next to her now.

Close…much too close, her brain informed her.

Too close not to notice how his brows crunched together like he was in deep thought, tense, or possibly irritated over something.

"What?" Chante asked, unable to control her rudeness.

If he insisted on taxing her, she would show him she wasn't taking any more of it.

About what happened earlier, I'm sorry, that was uncalled for," Jared apologized.

Chante was surprised by the unexpected apology. But she wasn't quite ready to give in yet.

"Oh, you mean groping my butt while your mom was peeing? I totally understand. I assume that's what you rich guys do," Chante replied in a voice dripping with sarcasm.

Jared sighed. Chante thought he looked really ashamed, but she wasn't sure. Guys like him were beyond her league.

"Tell me what I can do to make up for it…anything," Jared said earnestly.

Chante thought about it. If he was genuine, which she sincerely doubted, it was payback time.

"Kiss me then…so I can tell all the other nurses who have the hots for you what a lousy kisser you are," Chante replied.

She really just meant it as a joke. But looking back, she wondered where she got the sagacity to challenge him that way.

"Why you little imp…," Jared declared.

With one fast move, Chante found herself in his arms. His hands crossed around her waist, pulling her close. One hand reached up and grasped her chin firmly. Chante watched with a mixture of horror and fascination as his lips slowly descended down on hers. His breath wafted between parted lips.

Her initial reaction was to struggle, tell him she was just kidding, but the eyes that gazed deeply into hers had a hypnotic appeal. Chante felt her protest vanish as her knees turned to jelly. Her hands grasped the side of his hips to keep from falling.

His lips were warm and soft against hers, a gentle kiss meant to impart a message that he was a good kisser. But Chante was surprised by her own reaction as she opened her mouth slightly and bit him gently on the lower lip.

She heard the intake of breath at her audacity. Jared's tongue entered her mouth in a French kiss as his hands crept up to her breast and fondled them against the fabric of her uniform. Chante felt the world tilt around her feet. Her arms reached up, clasped the back of his neck to bring him even closer.

She felt his hand travel inside her blouse caressing her waist before travelling upward under her bra until she felt the warmth of his palm against her bare breast. His fingers searched her nipple and as he grasped it between his thumb and forefinger, Chante knew she was lost. The pleasure shot all the way to her groin.

"Jared…," she whispered huskily, recognizing the desire blooming between her thighs.

"Shhh…," Jared replied.

"Your mom…," Chante protested.

They won't be back yet…," Jared whispered before giving her a torrid kiss once more.

"We can't…not on the bed…," Chante protested horrified at the thought.

"I know…," Jared replied between her parted lips.

He reached down and hoisted her legs so that she straddled him upright. Then, without breaking a sweat, Jared carried her into the bathroom.

Once inside, he thrust her against the porcelain side of the wash basin as his mouth came down hard on hers once again. With the wall against her back and his entire body molded against hers, Chante felt his erection through the thin fabric of her dress. She wiggled her hips slightly, allowing her crotch to feel him.

His hands frantically searched for the zipper on her back, unzipped it, as Chante allowed the upper garment to fall against her lap. Her bra hung askew against her navel.

Jared's lips traveled down her neck and towards her ear. Chante could feel his ragged breathing as he lowered his mouth and gently sucked on her nipple. His hand groped her other breast as he rolled his palm and squeezed her.

Chante's arms wound their way around his neck in a frenzy. Every pore in her body screamed to be taken by this man. She could feel the rippling muscles on his chest as her hands feverishly tried to open his pants. She fondled him and felt the rocklike hardness of his penis as it reared free from its confines.

Chante knew they didn't have much time. The clandestine act was its own feverish thrill.

She pulled her pants down together with her thong panties and let them settle against her ankles. When Jared reached down beneath her, the touch of his fingers on her clit sent her body into a delicious spasm. He began to rub her…slowly, repeatedly and with controlled precise movement. She couldn't believe the heat that engulfed her. The hair on her skin stood on ends. She was on fire.

Jared stretched out his arms and used the wall to support him as Chante clung to his neck. With her hand around his penis, she positioned it against her notch, thrusting her pelvis towards him, feeling the rigid cock as it slowly entered her vagina.

Slowly at first, and then increasing his rhythm bit by bit, Jared explored and filled her entirely. Holding her down so he could feel her deep inside, Jared grunted like a beast in heat. Chante felt her orgasm explode inside, as with one last powerful thrust, Jared followed. He buried his face into her neck, back arched, body twitching with the remnants of his lust.

As their breathing subsided, Chante was struck with the enormity of what just happened. She never intended for things to come this far. She pushed him aside and pulled up her pants, struggling awkwardly to adjust her bra and fumbling with the zip on her blouse.

She had to get out of here. She had to put some distance between them. She hardly met his eyes as she opened the bathroom door, ignoring his voice calling out her name as she fled the room.

To hell with Director Whittle. She could make up an excuse for Nurse Betty why she disappeared. What she wanted right now was to crawl into a hole.

Damn Jared Lowell... The thought lingered for a few extra seconds as she ran into the night like the devil was in pursuit.

Chapter Three

Chante stared at her reflection in the bathroom mirror. Seven hours of sleep had restored her equilibrium. There was an undeniable sparkle in the emerald green eyes. She had a secret, one that she wouldn't ever have the guts to share with anyone. No one should ever know what transpired in a bathroom of a patient in NY General Hospital. And who would even believe her?

She felt like she won the lottery. Heck, this wasn't something she could add to her achievements in her resume. Still, the memory brought a smile to her face that she tried to hide from her brother, Markey.

"Why d'you look so happy?' Markey eyed her suspiciously.

Do I...? she responded nonchalantly.

"Maybe because I have called in sick and will be with you the next three days?" she answered and was gratified with a loud "whoopee."

She had decided on taking the spineless way out. She had no intentions of seeing Jared Lowell once again after what happened.

Whenever her conscience attacked her, she comforted herself with the thought, "We were two consenting adults, so it's fine…"

She hoped that when she returned to work, mother and son would have been gone.

"… transfer to some fancy health facility or wherever billionaires go to recover," Chante grumbled under her breath.

The idea made her feel despondent as her stomach plummeted.

"So what if I never see him again?" she asked herself.

But she did spend a lot of time on Google and was surprised at the stack of information there was about him.

"… Jared Lowell touted as one of America's most eligible bachelors…"

"…Scion of Jared Lowell, Sr. and Chairman of Lowell Enterprises that span three continents…"

"… Receiving his diploma from Harvard Business School…"

There were photos of him as a young boy atop a Shetland pony with sweeping long shots of mountain ranges behind him, and a more recent one with his arm slung carelessly across the shoulder of a stunning brunette.

Chante searched for information about the girl, but found none. Instead, she felt a stab of pain pierce her heart.

"So… he has a girlfriend…what did you expect? A guy like him probably has a girlfriend behind every door he opens, including bathroom doors," she grumbled under her breath.

She donned her scrubs hurriedly on the fourth day not wanting to be late again. She subdued the blooming optimism of seeing him again. Life would be so much simpler if both were gone by now.

The hospital entrance was swarming with paparazzi. Chante's heart skipped a beat. Unless a movie star or another celebrity was confined, this could only mean one thing. Jared Lowell was still in the building.

The funk she carried the last three days suddenly disappeared.

"At least I'll still get to see him… even from afar," she consoled herself.

Chante was willing to accept scraps at the moment.

She made her way hurriedly to the station on the second floor. Nurse Betty was handing out time patient charts to the other nurses. They all looked eagerly at the charts. Chante saw how each face fell with disappointment.

"I was hoping to get room 247...," one said.

Dream on bitch… I'm getting that today…," declared another.

I'll take a 24 hour shift, Nurse Betty, if you give me 247 now…," enthused another.

There was a lot of good-natured teasing among the ladies. Chante was doubtful Nurse Betty would give it to her after hasty retreat three days ago.

"Now… now… ladies, control your hormones. I do not need a cat fight right now. All of you… *go!*" Nurse Betty remarked sternly.

As the other nurses dispersed, Nurse Betty handed Chante a chart. And to her amazement, 247 were written clearly on the front.

"247 again…?" Chante remarked.

It was difficult to control the sudden wild hammering in her heart. She tried to appear nonchalant, but the sparkle in her eyes didn't fool the Head Nurse.

"I never play favorites, you know that... I wanted you nurse bitches to draw lots… Heck, I would have pulled hair and gouge an eye to get a chance to be near that stud in 247, but there was nothing I could do. He asked for you, Chante," Nurse Betty said.

"He asked for me?" Chante echoed.

Her knees turned to jelly.

"Samantha Lowell is a VIP patient. Her son Jared happens to be the biggest donor to the Hospital Trust

Fund. So you can understand Director Jonathan Whittle will give him a witch-doctor or a shaman if he asks for it," the head nurse explained.

It was not easy to control her trembling body as Chante walked the floor towards room 247. With a soft knock, she turned the doorknob and entered softly.

She hardly recognized the room from three days ago. It has transformed into a virtual office. Three telephone lines stood on a console table that was brought in. Two technicians were installing a satellite dish by the window as another crew put the finishing touches on a wide-screen TV mounted on the wall.

Jared Lowell sat upright on a table with a powered-up Mac before him. He was talking into a dicta-phone. He stopped momentarily when he saw her enter. A hint of a smile lit up his face.

"You're late…," he said.

Chante wanted to contradict him as she glanced at her wrist watch. It showed the time at 9:09. Her shift started at 9:00a.m.

"We're sorry for all of these," Mrs. Lowell said, waving her hand over the entire room. "This was the only way he could get any work done while I'm in the hospital…," she explained.

Chante approached her, asked how she was feeling, took her temperature and pulse reading, and administered her medication. She was still a nurse, albeit a befuddled one.

The old woman's cell phone rang and Chante moved away to give her some privacy.

As Mrs. Lowell retrieved her phone, Chante took the time to study her chart. Jared casually sauntered to where she stood. His presence was electric, hard to ignore, especially since her heart was racing.

"Are you planning on staying forever," she muttered under her breath indicating the room which now looked more like an office.

She meant it as a casual comment but came out like a snide remark.

"Would you like me to go…?" Jared asked, with a hurt expression in his eyes.

'No… no… no… sorry, I just meant…," Chante stuttered.

She realized she had no explanation and like the coward she was, she fled the room…again.

Chapter Four

For the next few hours Chante switched charts with some of the nurses who couldn't believe their luck. She needed to stay away from him. Chante wanted to salvage whatever dignity she had. He always managed to make her feel like a bumbling idiot. She was no match for him, she accepted that. She hoped Nurse Betty wouldn't notice.

Just then a commotion ensued at the Nurse's station. One of the girls Chante persuaded to take over just returned crying.

"What's wrong?" Chante asked.

"He's having a temper tantrum… refused to let me take the patient's pulse and temperature… almost threw me out of the room…," the girl sobbed.

Chante was aghast. She imagined what that was like. The guy was obviously a billionaire spoiled brat. But she wasn't ready to go in there yet. She got the chart and passed it on to another nurse, hoping she'd accept it. The girl didn't want it either, tossing the chart back to her like it were biohazard.

Oh…alright…I'll do it," she grumbled as four sets of eyes looked at her retreating back with concern.

Chante knocked and entered with some hesitation.

"Oh, Chante, thank God…," Mrs. Lowell cried, waving her in. Her son was by her side with a contrite expression.

"Mr. Lowell…," she began.

"Jared…," he cut in.

"Mr. Lowell, why…," she tried again.

"Jared…," he repeated.

Chante sighed.

"Jared then… why are you being difficult?" she asked him.

"It was the only way I knew to make you come back," he replied, with a smug look.

Mrs. Lowell gave an exasperated sigh and remarked, "My dear, can you please bring my son somewhere else. Get some air. As much as I adore him, he is getting into my nerves."

Oh Jesus. This wasn't in her job description.

"Ok…," she answered meekly.

It was obvious that the confinement was wearing them both down.

"Are you sure you'll be alright, mom. We'll just get a bite to eat," Jared asked.

"Go…go…go…," Mrs. Lowell answered.

Chante felt her heart soar, but refused to think more of it. This was a request from a VIP patient. How could she say no? But she knew exactly where she could take him. Breath of fresh air? Check.

Outside the hall, she walked ahead of him. If he wanted to come he would surely follow. Jared pulled her back and slipped his fingers between hers.

"Jared, please…," Chante protested, pulling away from him.

But he pulled back again and kept his fingers entwined with hers.

"Jared, please…" She was almost begging.

The touch of his hand on hers was setting her body on fire.

"If I promise to behave, you won't run away again?" he asked.

Chante accepted the truce. Deep inside anxiety bloomed. The flirtation was exciting. But it would not lead to anything. Not with someone like him.

Chante steered clear of the Nurses' Station where the elevators were situated. She didn't want to start another hullabaloo with the nurses. She pushed towards the freight elevator located at the end of the hall.

The elevator took them to the top floor of NYC General Hospital. Few people were about as Chante pressed on toward a set of metal doors at the rear. She twisted the handle and pushed outward.

Dusk had descended on New York City as Chante led Jared towards the railing of the roof deck. A few stars struggled to make their presence felt. Buildings dotted Manhattan like a shroud spread out below. The sky was a dazzling shade of lavender and crimson against an orange sun descending slowly in the horizon.

A comfortable silence ensued. No words necessary to describe the magnificent splendor unfolding before them.

The electricity between them was harder to explain.

Chante wondered how many times he had seen this postcard setting with a girl beside him. She'd seen it often enough whenever she wanted to escape the drama of the hospital floor. Surprisingly for her, today it felt like the first time because he was by her side.

Why did he affect her the way he did? Was it the casual sex they shared? He must be an expert in the game of seduction. She wasn't. She tried to stay away and he didn't like that. Was she expected to play along? She didn't know the answer.

Chante pushed the complicated thoughts aside as Jared stirred beside her.

"Thank you, Chante Green, CNA…," he muttered softly.

The naughty look was back in his face. She watched him turn slowly towards her like a movie reel in her mind.

Chante stepped into his embrace. His arms snaked their way around her waist and pulled her near. She savored the intimacy and closed her eyes. It felt amazing. Their bodies were a perfect fit.

When Jared's lips descended on her, Chante thought the sky lit up with fireworks like the Fourth of July. In that single moment, she was willing to take any chances.

"I like you, Chante…a lot. There's something different about you," Jared said, his chin resting softly on the top of her head.

Chante smiled secretly. That was a good start.

"I'd like to see you more…," Jared continued.

Chante thought she was dreaming.

And then he added, "I was wondering…you know…I want to set you up somewhere, a condo maybe …I want you to stop working at the hospital so I can see you anytime I'm free from all the work I have to do…I can buy you stuff…girls like that, right? You're free to do anything you want when I'm not around. See your friends, watch movies, go to the theater, but I want you to be with me exclusively, just me…no hanky-panky when I'm not around."

Chante froze.

"You want me to be your mistress?" she asked with a shocked look on her face.

"I don't do the boyfriend-girlfriend thing…," Jared replied hesitantly.

He couldn't understand the look of horror on her face.

Chante felt like she had just been doused with ice water. Did he even know what he was saying? Everything he said was "I want…I want…," with no regard for what she wanted. Didn't do the boyfriend-girlfriend thing? What was she to be in his life? A sex toy? And once he got tired of her… what then? Would he casually drop her just like his casual invitation to be his kept woman?

Chante stepped back and drew away from him. The look on her face was undeniable, like he just insulted her beyond belief.

"What? What did I do wrong?" Jared asked perplexed.

He really thought she would be ecstatic with his proposition. She seemed to like him a lot. She gave all the right signals. This was the first time a girl reacted the way she did. Mostly, they were only too happy to accept that kind of arrangement.

Chante could hardly speak.

"I'm not that kind of girl," Chante whispered through stiff lips, "I'm not a whore that you picked up on the street."

"Have I ever treated you like one?" Jared asked.

"You just did…," Chante whispered back.

Despite her promise she would not run away again, Chante fled.

The happiness she felt over their kiss had turned into lead that weighed a tonne inside her. She was right the first time. There was no future in that direction. He was offering her a temporary haven that would eventually find her out in the cold once the curiosity dwindled.

She couldn't accept that. Not now that she was confronted with the truth. She was in love with him. His proposition made that realization so much harder to admit. For her sake, she had to forget him.

Forget he didn't see her for who she really was… forget that he thought his money could buy him the affection that she wanted to give him freely, not in exchange for "stuff" he mentioned.

She had to break free. Break the barriers she inadvertently built around her heart when she first laid eyes on Jared Lowell.

Without saying another word, Chante turned around, leaving Jared open-mouthed and wide eyed. As she left the rooftop, she closed the door behind her.

-To be continued in Book 2-

If you enjoyed this title, I would appreciate your leaving a review of the book. Good reviews encourage an author to write as well as help books to sell. Good reviews can be just a few short sentences describing what you liked about the book without having a spoiler. If you could spend 30 seconds writing a review, I would appreciate it: you can review this title right now at your favorite retailer.

Here is a preview of the **next book** you may also enjoy:

"**ARE WE** doing spring cleaning?" Markey Green asked his sister Chante as he eyed the clothes strewn all over her bedroom floor.

"What? No…no…no…" Chante replied, as she pulled another hanger from inside her clothes drawer.

"I just need to find the right one…" she added as she positioned the dress in front of her and stared at her reflection in the mirror.

She shook her head in disapproval. "Too revealing," she muttered under her breathe.

Markey advanced slowly into his sister's bedroom. He didn't want his wheelchair to run into the dresses that were piled haphazardly on the floor.

"Must be a hot date then," he smiled with amusement as his sister began to attack the shelves where her shoes rested.

Chante stopped momentarily. She was surprised at her brother's spontaneous perception. She smiled trying to mask the concern in her eyes. He had grown so much thinner these last few months. His ALS had progressed so much faster than she thought.

"And what do you know about having a hot date, hmmm…" she said as she tousled his hair.

"Well…enough to notice that you're excited once again. These last few months you just seemed… sad." Markey replied.

Chante felt a twinge of guilt. She honestly didn't realize her brother noticed at all.

"Was I that bad…" she asked as she sat down on the bed.

"Bad? Nah, you were just sad." Markey answered wryly.

"Yeah, I guess I was…but I'm ok now…so don't you worry about me kid." Chante replied.

She never told him about the way she felt. In fact she hasn't told anyone about it. Who would believe her anyway? It isn't everyday that a good-looking and wealthy… very wealthy… Jared Lowell asked you to be his sex toy.

Chante tried to forget everything that happened that day on the roof deck of NY General Hospital. She remembered him calling her name as she pushed the metal doors aside and ran towards the freight elevator. She punched the button on the lift and went all the way to the basement where she knew she would be safe. She was confused, her mind was in a whirl, and she wanted to stay away from prying eyes. She stopped by a wall and there amidst rows of empty cars she slumped down on the hard cement floor as despair and disillusionment brought waves of tears that shook her to the core.

"How dare him…" she muttered disconsolately, "he must think I'm scum."

Jared Lowell, heir to the fortunes of Lowell Enterprises had just offered to keep her as a mistress in exchange for a condo and for "stuff" as he called it, even having the impudence to conclude "that's what girls like…"

But Chante didn't have the heart to put all the censure on the scoundrel. She was partly to blame too, remembering what happened between them in the bathroom of the suite where his mother was a patient.

"Shit…" she whispered between her tears.

But it was too late now for regrets. It happened and she had to live with it. In hindsight, she was confused why she even allowed it to come about. Had the patient, Samantha Lowell, or Nurse Betty, and Director Whittle come back and caught them in the illicit act, she would have lost her job as Certified Nursing Assistant, that's for sure.

It was with uncertainty that she reported for work the very next day. She had vowed the night before that she would refuse adamantly, beg even, not to be assigned to Suite 247 once again. But the floor seemed unusually quiet that morning. She learned that Samantha Lowell was discharged the night before. The private helicopter that brought her in brought her out, as well.

"Oh, thank God," was Chante's initial reaction.

She didn't have to suffer the awkwardness of seeing Jared again. Admittedly, she liked Mrs. Lowell. She felt a certain degree of kinship with the older woman. It made her a little sad, thinking she didn't get a chance to say goodbye.

But as the initial relief swept through her body, she was also assailed with a deep sense of melancholy. She won't be seeing Jared Lowell anymore. That, at least, was its own blessing, Chante thought.

The weeks that followed their departure, Chante often had to struggle with her feelings. She tried to focus on her work but often found herself looking out into space. She felt miserable, disconnected, and it took all her effort to keep going about her duty. The world lay heavily on her shoulders.

Nurse Betty took her aside and asked what was bothering her. Chante couldn't look her in the eye. The woman was very perceptive.

"Is this about a man?" Nurse Betty inquired.

Chante nodded her head. The supervisor didn't have to know who. So Chante decided on a half-lie.

"Yes…but it's over now…" Chante answered.

"That's good. If it didn't last too long, then he must be the wrong guy for you. Get out of that hole you crawled into. Someone better should come along for you." The supervisor consoled her.

Chante nodded her head in agreement. Nurse Betty didn't know how close to the truth she was. Jared

Lowell was definitely the wrong guy for her. It's about time she moved on and forgot all about him.

Things were slowly getting back to normal.

If you enjoyed this sample then look for **Love Astray: Audacious Billionaire BWWM Romance Series, Book 2**.

Here is a preview of **another story** you may enjoy:

Love Disrupted - Ardent Billionaire Romance Series, Book 1

DEIRDRE CLARKE stepped out of her apartment into the hot Los Angeles sun; dusk had fallen, but the temperature still sat near 100 degrees. Deirdre was already running late for her gig, so the sight of her ex-boyfriend Carl standing by her car irritated her even more than usual. She stomped down the single flight of stairs and greeted him with hostility.

"I'm late. What the hell do you want?" Deirdre demanded.

"Can't a man just stop by to see his best girl?" Carl smiled. His green eyes complimented his mocha skin and for a moment Deirdre forgot why she'd put up with his shit for so long. Then she remembered why she'd stopped.

"I guess you'd better go see her then," she said roughly. "And let me be on my way."

"Dee… you know I'm talking about you."

"I'm not your girl no more," she answered, "and I've got somewhere to be."

"Don't be mad, Dee I just came here to check on you… you alright? What about D'Angelo? You two need anything? You got rent covered?"

Deirdre's blood boiled and she met his eyes with a defiant stare. "I don't need a damn thing from you. D'Angelo and I are not your business anymore." Deirdre had been responsible for her younger brother since their mother had gone to prison. D'Angelo was one of the reasons she'd known she had to get away from Carl in the first place. The last thing she wanted was for her brother to see her thug ex-boyfriend as a role model.

"When are you going to understand that you can't buy your way back here?" She glared at him.

"Deirdre, we were together almost our whole lives. I love you. But I'm not trying to buy my way back. I have a business proposition for you."

"I don't need a job, I have two," she snapped, trying to open her car door. Carl blocked her way.

"Its easy money Dee… you wouldn't even know it was here."

"Ah, I see. You think I'll hide drugs or hot shit for you, after all of the hell you put me through? You think I'd take that risk for you and your 'boys'?" She snorted back at him.

"It's just herb, Dee… it's practically legal. And I don't know why you're so pissed at me. Nothing that went down was my FAULT!"

"Our windows were SHOT OUT, Carl. You can stand there all you want and claim it was a random drive-by, swear it wasn't personal, but I'm not a moron! You think I didn't know you'd fallen in with Derrick and his thugs? You think I believed your lies about where all the money was coming from? I KNEW what you were doing, and you just denied, denied, denied.

Until our home was shot up... with my brother inside. Take your shit and get out of my face." Deirdre shoved him out of the way of her car and escaped inside. She checked her face in the rearview mirror, and then prayed she'd have time to fix her make-up before she had to go onstage.

She stood on stage, in her element. As Lou played along on the black grand piano, Deirdre let all of her emotions flow out to the music. The small crowd gave her their undivided attention as she belted out Trouble, Stormy Weather, and Summertime. Her white, full length gown stood in stark contrast to the milk-chocolate color of her skin.

Deirdre couldn't remember a time when she didn't love to sing. When she was still a young girl, before her father left, her family went to church every Sunday. She loved listening to the soloists in the choir and dreamed of one day standing next to them. But they'd stopped going to church once her father was gone. When D'Angelo was born, Deirdre had tried to get her mother to go back, but she'd refused; D'Angelo's father was against the idea. But soon, he was gone too. Looking back, Deirdre was sure that was when her mother started using drugs, though she didn't realize what was happening at the time. Three years ago, right after Deirdre graduated from high-school, Pauline Clarke had been busted and sentenced to twenty years in a federal prison. Deirdre became D'Angelo's legal guardian, though in all honesty she'd raised him since he was born.

D'Angelo was a good kid, especially considering everything he'd been through. And he was the reason Deirdre hadn't fallen into the same kind of traps the other girls in her neighborhood had found themselves in. She hadn't had any kids, she hadn't gotten messed up on drugs, and she didn't take her clothes off for money. Instead, Deirdre worked as a hotel maid and took college courses online. She'd have loved to go to school on an actual campus, but she couldn't afford childcare for D'Angelo and she refused to turn him into a latchkey kid at eight years old. Deirdre worked while he was at school, and then after dinner they did their homework together.

Thursday nights were different. Those nights were all for Deirdre. She had a standing gig at Fuseli's, an upscale jazz club in the Hollywood foothills. The gig paid just enough for Deirdre to afford her stage-clothes, but she didn't do it for the money.

When she finished her last set, Deirdre took a seat at the bar and ordered herself a beer and a sandwich. As the bartender walked towards the tap, a tall, broad stranger signaled his attention. When he returned to Deirdre, he carried a martini with her draft.

"Dee, a kind gentleman asked me to bring you this and wondered if you'd mind some company?"

Deirdre looked up at Steve and sighed. After her encounter with Carl, she was in no mood to put up with anyone's advances. "Tell him thank you, but I can't possibly accept."

"I don't know… this one's pretty hot, Dee… he's the one down there, in the suit."

"Really Steve, I'm not up for it right now."

"Alright, fine…" he answered in a disapproving, sing-song voice.

Deirdre thought the issue was dealt with as she watched Steve approach the end of the bar to deliver the message. The gorgeous blonde man took the martini, rose, and headed Deirdre's way.

"I'm sorry," she began as he approached, frustrated that he wouldn't take a hint.

"No, I'm sorry." He smiled. "Your friend told me you've had a bad day. You sang beautifully… I sent this as a token of my appreciation, nothing more," he explained, raising the drink. "Why don't you enjoy it? It might make you feel better. Or I could buy you something else, if you'd prefer? Right before I return to my seat, of course."

If you enjoyed this sample then look for **Love Disrupted - Ardent Billionaire Romance Series, Book 1**.

Here is a preview of **another story** you may enjoy:

Love Anew - Lonely Billionaire Romance Series, Book 1

TRICIA REACHED for another blanket. "Are you cold?" she asked.

Rebecca's breath was raspy as she responded. As her lungs shut down due to ALS, or Amyotrophic Lateral Sclerosis, her ability to speak had started to decline. Muscle by muscle, ALS targeted the body and made it impossible for the individual to live a normal life. It had started a few years ago with Rebecca's legs. Now, her lung muscles were starting to freeze as well. Tricia winced as she thought about the future. If Rebecca chose to use machines to stay alive, her entire body would eventually stop working. At some point, her mind would remain functioning and she would be locked into her body.

Rebecca managed to squeeze out a feeble yes. Reaching over to the cupboard, Tricia removed a blanket and carefully tucked her in. Tricia had spent years training to be a nurse and really liked her job. Since she was an excellent nurse, she had caught the eye of the billionaire, John, at one of the couple's many trips to hospitals around the country. He had noticed the love and care she took with each patient. After a moment's hesitation, Tricia had allowed him to convince her to take care of his wife.

Pictures of Rebecca dotted the room. Since she was unable to leave, John had striven to make her room look like favorite memories of her life and activities. A young, healthy Rebecca smiled in each photo. In the few years she had been physically active, she had acquired awards for horseback riding, cooking and other projects. Now, though, this time of physical fitness had passed. Instead of dashing through the fields on her favorite horse, Rebecca spent her time in this room. She had taken her difficulties in stride and was truly brave in the face of all of these medical issues.

Finishing with the blanket, Rebecca started to say something. Leaning closer to hear her, Tricia finally pulled up a chair. "What do you need, Rebecca?" she queried.

Sighing, Rebecca whispered, "I need to talk to John. I have to tell him how I want to die."

Squeezing her hand, Tricia nodded. "Once I leave your room, I will go get him. Just in case he is not around, did you want me to give him a message?"

Rebecca tried to nod, but her head did not respond all the way. "Yes, I do. You need to tell him that I do not want any machines. He could keep me alive forever with a breathing tube, but I do not want to live a life where I am permanently locked into my body. And," she paused and struggled to take another breath. "I do not want him to stop enjoying life or waiting around for my eventual death. If God wants to take my soul now, we should not interfere."

Tricia nodded sadly. Most patients with ALS were more afraid of being stuck within their minds than actual death. She understood, but she could not imagine what life would be like without Rebecca's gentle soul. "I will tell him," she said.

Leaving the room, Tricia traversed the hallways of the mansion. John had built his fortune by buying and selling real estate properties. His initial money had arrived through an early investment in the dot com boom before the bubble burst. After seeing the dangers of the stock market, he had started to just buy and rent out properties. Even with the recent recession, he still made a profit. Instead of selling his properties or developing, he had continued to rent them out. In a decade or two, he had talked of selling and retiring. His plans had arrived before his wife had been diagnosed with ALS. Unwilling to speak of his life after her future death, Tricia had not asked about any change in his future plans.

The halls of the house were dotted with white oak doorways that led to a myriad of rooms. Plush white carpet softly surrounded Tricia's feet as she walked. She dreaded the conversation that was about to happen. Every day, she updated John about the status of his wife. Unfortunately, she seldom had good news to share. She nodded to John's secretary as she entered the office. Unlike most rich men, he used a male secretary. Before talking had become so difficult, Rebecca had explained that he tried to hire primarily males so that Rebecca would never worry about his fidelity. Since Tricia was intended to cater just to his wife, she had been allowed to work there despite her gender.

If you enjoyed this sample then look for **Love Anew - Lonely Billionaire Romance Series, Book 1.**

Other Books by Shyla Starr

- Persuasive Billionaire BWWM Romance Series

- Tenacious Billionaire BWWM Romance Series

- Elusive Billionaire Romance Series

- Lonely Billionaire Romance Series

- Ardent Billionaire Romance Series

- Fervent Billionaire BWWM Romance Series

Get the latest update on new releases from the author at:

https://shylastarr.com/newsletter/

About the Author - Shyla Starr

Shyla currently specializes in writing interracial romance stories and is a huge fan of the alpha male. Simply put, there just aren't enough stories about mixed couple romances, which is something she is aiming to fix.

Being a bookworm all her life, when Shyla discovered men she also realized how easy it was to fulfill her fantasies through her writing.

When not writing and fantasizing about men, Shyla enjoys dancing, reading and chilling with her friends.

Connect with Shyla Starr

I really appreciate you reading my book! Here are my social media coordinates:

Friend me on Facebook: https://www.facebook.com/shylastarrauthor

Follow me on Twitter: https://twitter.com/shylstarr

Check me out on Goodreads: https://www.goodreads.com/author/show/8436084.Shyla_Starr

Subscribe to my newsletter: https://shylastarr.com/newsletter/

Visit my website: https://shylastarr.com/